Winnie the Pooh's

Book of Manners

Winnie the Pooh's
Book of Manners

MARY HOGAN

ILLUSTRATED BY JOHN KURTZ

NEW YORK

For Mom and Dad, with love and thanks—M.H.

I dedicate this book to my wife, Sandrina, who thinks of others
before herself and always, always tells the truth.—J.K.

Printed in the United States of America.
Based on the Pooh stories by A. A. Milne (copyright © The Pooh Properties Trust).
FIRST EDITION
1 3 5 7 9 10 8 6 4 2
Library of Congress Catalog Card Number: 98-86109
ISBN: 0-7868-3206-1

CONTENTS

Manners Matter

One bright morning in the Hundred-Acre Wood, Winnie the Pooh met up with his good friend Christopher Robin.

"Hello, Christopher Robin," called Pooh. "What do you have there?" Pooh could not help noticing that his friend was carrying a round honeypot. *That's just the sort of honeypot to keep honey in,* thought the honey-loving bear excitedly.

"This is for you, Pooh," said Christopher Robin, giving his friend the pot filled with honey.

"Yummy!" cried Pooh.

Then he said, "Mmmm."

Then he said, "Aaahh."

There was something that Pooh remembered he was forgetting to say. But what was it?

Pooh said, "Mmmm!" one more time—which is a perfectly fine thing to say (Pooh said it as often as he could), but "Mmmm" didn't seem to be the perfectly fine thing to say to Christopher Robin.

After a while, Christopher Robin began poking a stick at a hole in the ground. "You do know what manners are, right, Pooh Bear?" he asked.

"Oh, of course," said Pooh quickly. He shook the fluff and stuffing in his brain, but nothing quite like "manners" seemed to be up there. "Do you mean the small or largish

manners, exactly?"

"Manners are usually small," said Christopher Robin thoughtfully. "But they have a largish sort of meaning to them."

"Just what I thought, too," said Pooh. "And what was that meaning, again?"

"Manners," said Christopher Robin, "are the ways that we treat each other. They are the things we do and say that tell others that we care about them."

"You mean like sharing a pot of honey with a friend?" said Pooh.

"Yes," said Christopher Robin.

"And saying . . ." Pooh tapped his head, think-think-think. "And saying thank you to a sharing friend?"

"Yes," said Christopher Robin.

"Thank you, Christopher Robin," said Pooh.

"You're welcome, Pooh
Bear," said Christopher
Robin.

And then, without even
a hum-de-dum or a dum-de-
hum, Pooh discovered that

he had a whole new hum just ready to roll out—all about
pleases and thank-yous:

If a bear wants honey
(Of course! Each day!),
then "please" is the special thing to say.
If someone shares
(Hooray! Happy tummy!),
then a bear says "Thank you." And "Mmm, yummy!"

Going Visiting

Looking up at the racing clouds over the Wood, Pooh Bear had a thought. He didn't often have them, so it was in a somewhat surprised voice that he asked his friend Christopher Robin, "Do you think Piglet knows about manners? It might be a friendly sort of reason for a visit."

"Very friendly," agreed Christopher Robin, and the two set off.

"If we got there right at eleven-o'clockish, he might offer us a smackerel or two," added Pooh hopefully. "And I would say 'thank you.'"

"Good idea, Pooh," said Christopher Robin. "We can practice all our manners."

It wasn't long before the winding path through the Hundred-Acre Wood brought the friends right up to the beech tree where Piglet lived.

Pooh knocked on the door.

"Who is it?" asked Piglet.

"It's me," said Pooh. "Who are you?"

"I'm me, too," said Piglet, surprised. "But you sound just like Winnie the Pooh."

"It is Pooh—and Christopher Robin," said Christopher Robin.

"Oh, welcome," said Piglet, opening the door. "Please come in."

Christopher Robin held the door for Pooh. They both wiped their feet on the mat.

"How do you do?" asked Pooh.

"I'm fine, thank you," said Piglet. "How are you, Pooh Bear?"

"Fine, thank you," said Pooh. "'Thank you' is a useful expression, isn't it?"

"Oh, very useful," agreed Piglet.

Pooh sighed contentedly. "Just as I thought."

"Would you like a little something to eat?" asked Piglet.

"Little or large, either one," said Pooh. Then he paused—that didn't sound quite like good manners. "I mean, yes, please."

Pooh waited his turn for some of Piglet's honey
sandwiches. "Thank you, Piglet."

Pooh took only the smaller sandwiches—to make sure
there were enough for his friends. He even remembered not
to lick his plate when he was done.

Then Piglet told a story about looking for haycorns. Pooh knew a useful fact about haycorns, but he didn't interrupt.

"Haycorns are often found near haycorn trees—but sometimes not," said Pooh, after Piglet was finished with his story.

Christopher Robin and Pooh helped clean up, and threw their crumbs away.

"Good-bye, Piglet," said Pooh. "Thank you for the sandwiches."

"You're welcome," said Piglet. "I'll see you at Roo's party tonight."

And as the two friends walked off through the woods, a new hum buzz-buzzed in the brain of Pooh.

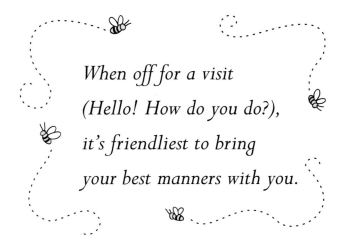

When off for a visit
(Hello! How do you do?),
it's friendliest to bring
your best manners with you.

Playing Games

Christopher Robin and Pooh hadn't traveled very far along
the rambling path in the Hundred-Acre Wood when they
heard a familiar voice.

"I know who *hoo-hoo* and *hoo*s like that," said Pooh.

And with a bounce and a bump, Pooh found himself looking right up at Tigger.

"Hiya, Buddy Bear!" said Tigger. "Terrifically bouncety day for a bounce, don't ya agree? Hoo-hoo-*hoo*!"

"A little too bouncety for a bear," said Pooh with a sigh.

"Too bouncety?" asked Tigger. "Is that possibibble?"

"All tiggers love bouncing," explained Christopher Robin. "But not all pooh bears love being bounced."

"Most interestin'," said Tigger, surprised.

"Good manners are mostly about looking at things from someone else's point of view," explained Christopher Robin.

"How do things look down there?" Tigger asked Pooh,
still sitting on top of his round friend.

"Kind of orange and . . . stripedy," said Pooh.

"Say, you're lookin' at things exactackily like a tigger!" cheered Tigger. "But you're not the onliest one wit' manners. Let me help ya up."

"Thank you, Tigger," said Pooh.

"Furthermost, Pooh Bear, I am most sorrily sorry for this and all those tiggerific future bounces sure an' certain to come your way," offered Tigger.

"Oh bother," said Pooh.

"I mean, thank you, Tigger."

"How 'bout I make it up to ya with a game o' Pooh Sticks," suggested Tigger. "I've found some extry-speediforous sticks just right for racin'."

"All right," agreed Pooh.

"I'm going to read my book in that shady spot," said
Christopher Robin. "Have fun!"

Tigger shared his new sticks with Pooh.

The friends tossed their sticks off the side of the bridge. Then they raced to the other side to see whose stick would be the first to pass under the bridge.

They played a little more quietly than usual today
so they wouldn't bother Christopher Robin.

"Pooh Sticks are what tiggers do best," bragged Tigger. Then he looked at his friend. Good manners had a way of bouncing from one person to the other. "Pooh Bears are pretty terrifical, too," he added.

"There's my stick!" said Pooh happily. "I win!"

"Let's play again," said Tigger.

Tigger loved playing Pooh
Sticks, but he loved it most
when he won. So when Pooh
said, "Ready . . . set . . . "
Tigger threw his stick.

"And throw!" finished Pooh,
and threw in his own stick.

Soon Tigger's stick
appeared at the other side of
the bridge. It was ahead of
Pooh's stick, but Tigger didn't
quite feel like a winner.

"Let's play that one again," said Tigger. "My stick had a bit of a twitchy feel about it."

"Okay," agreed Pooh. He had thought Tigger's toss looked a little twitchy (in a there-it-goes-and-I-haven't-quite-called-throw-yet kind of way). But Pooh hadn't wanted to say so.

The friends tossed sticks again, right at the same time. Pooh's came out ahead again. "Good goin' there," Tigger said, giving his friend's paw a shake, but looking a little down around the whiskers all the same.

Pooh looked at his remaining sticks. One was decorated with a bright green bud. "I think this is a lucky sort of Pooh Stick," said Pooh. "Do you want to try with this one?"

"Why, thanks, Buddy Bear," said Tigger, cheering right up. And soon Tigger's stick, with the lucky green bud, had won the very next race.

"Well done, Tigger," said Pooh Bear.

"Hoo-hoo-*hoo*!" hooted Tigger. "Playin' fair an' square is what tiggers—and poohs—do best."

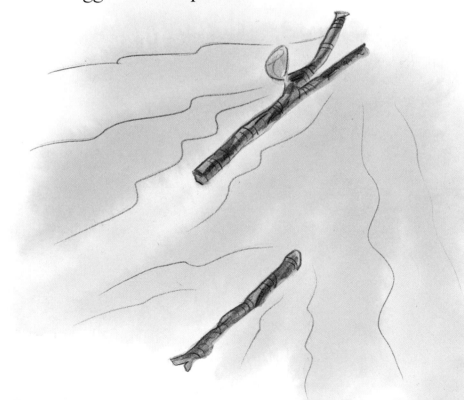

"It's time!" called Christopher Robin.

"Oh, good," said Pooh. "Time for what?"

"Time to go to our homes and get ready for Roo's party,"
said Christopher Robin.

"Oh," said Pooh. "I thought you were going to say it was time for a hum."

"It might be time for that, too," said Christopher Robin. And it was.

Playing fair and square
(thrum-dum, this hum's begun)
isn't just friendly manners—
it makes the game more fun!

Going to a Party

Everyone in the Hundred-Acre Wood was invited to Roo's birthday party. Kanga and Roo hadn't forgotten a single friend.

A Party for Roo

When: 2:00 P.M. Wednesday

Where: Kanga and Roo's house

Wear: No fancy clothes required

Please let Kanga know if you cannot come.

At his home, Pooh looked at the invitation that Kanga had sent him. Christopher Robin had drawn a picture of a clock on it, so he would know just when to be there.

Pooh would have to hurry if he was going to clean up and still be on time for the party.

Pooh washed his face and paws carefully and put on a clean red shirt.

I hope Roo likes his present, thought Pooh.

Pooh himself liked presents of the honeypot or smackerel-of-honey or some-kind-of-honey sort, but Roo didn't like honey quite as much as Pooh did.

Roo liked colorful pictures. So Pooh had made Roo a special picture of the picnic they had together. Pooh used his nearest-to-new crayons and his best paper. Pooh carefully rolled up the picture and wrapped a bright ribbon around it.

Now it was time to go! Hurrying through the Wood, Pooh almost didn't . . . but then he did. Yes, he definitely heard the buzz-buzzing of honeybees in the trees.

I don't think honeybees would buzz-buzz like that if they weren't making especially yummy honey, thought Pooh. He listened again.

He might be able to jump over that mud puddle,

clamber through those pricker bushes,

and climb up the tree for a quick
pawful of sweet, golden . . .

"Hello!" called a voice.

"Hello!" said Pooh. "Are you calling me, honey tree?"

"Pooh, it's me—Piglet," said Piglet. Pooh looked down. His little friend was headed up the path toward him.

"Oh, hello, Piglet," said Pooh. "Why were you pretending to be a honey tree?"

"Was I?" said Piglet. "Oh, dear. I must have pretended so well that I fooled myself. But I am a piglet. Aren't I, Pooh?"

"The very best piglet I know," Pooh assured his friend.

"Thank you, Pooh," said Piglet happily. "Are you going to Roo's party now?"

"Oh, yes," said Pooh. "I was just telling this honey tree that I would have to visit it later—perhaps tomorrow, around lunchtime. Right now, I'm on my way to a party, and I can't be late."

"We had better hurry," suggested Piglet.

"Is there time for a hum?" asked Pooh.

"Is there a piglet in the hum?" asked Piglet shyly.

"Maybe just a little one," said Pooh.

"Ooh," said Piglet, turning a deeper shade of pink. "I think we have enough time."

Pooh hummed his hum:

Getting ready for a party:
washing, wrapping, with a smile.
Remember, if a honey tree calls,
call back, "I'll see you . . . after a while!"
And if that tree turns out to be
a piglet kind of friend,
it's best to join your paws
and walk together till the end.

Setting the Table

Right on time for the big birthday party, Piglet and Pooh arrived at Kanga and Roo's house.

"Hello, presents, er, I mean Piglet and Pooh," said Roo. His eyes were glued to the gifts in their hands. "Are those for me?"

"Roo, dear," said Kanga. "Is that how we welcome our guests?"

"Oops, sorry, Mama," said Roo. "Thank you for coming, Pooh and Piglet."

"These presents are for you," said Pooh and Piglet, giving their gifts to Roo.

"Hooray!" cheered Roo. He unrolled the picture from Pooh. "It's our picnic! What a wonderful picture! Thanks, Pooh."

"You're welcome," said Pooh cheerfully. Roo hung the picture up on the wall so everyone could see it.

Then Roo unwrapped the present from Piglet.

"It's . . . haycorn jam," said Roo.

Roo did not like haycorn jam very much, but he did like Piglet very much. "Thank you for the present," he said kindly.

"Let's put it out on the table so everyone can have some."

Kanga and Roo's house was filling with guests. Owl, Eeyore, and Christopher Robin were sitting at the table eating cookies.

"Pooh, dear, I was wondering if you could help me with an important job," said Kanga. "I was going to ask Rabbit, but he sent a note saying that he would be late."

"Important job?" said Pooh importantly. "I'd like to help."

"Thank you, Pooh. I just don't have time to set the table myself," said Kanga. She gave Pooh a large basket of knives, forks, spoons, and plates. Napkins were piled at the bottom.

Pooh carried the basket out to the picnic table. A pretty cloth covered the table.

Christopher Robin followed his friend outside. "Do you

remember how to set the table?" he asked.

"Oh, yes," replied Pooh. "But I remember it better when you show me."

"First we put the plate down in the middle," explained Christopher Robin. "On the left side of the plate, we put the fork. On the right side, we put the knife and spoon. A cup or glass goes above the knife. A napkin goes under the fork."

"That's just how I would do it, too," said Pooh.

"Sometimes at fancy parties, they have lots more of everything on the table," said Christopher Robin.

"Oh bother!" cried Pooh.

"Don't worry, Pooh Bear," said Christopher Robin. "When it's time to eat at a fancy table, you just start with the fork, spoon, and knife that are farthest from your plate."

"What a lovely table!" exclaimed Kanga. She carried out the cake, and all the guests followed her. "Thank you for helping me, Pooh."

"Christopher Robin helped me," explained Pooh.

"Of course he did," said Kanga. "That's the way it is with helping."

Piglet was impressed with the table, too. "How did you do it, Pooh?"

And this is what Pooh replied:

Plate in the middle,
knife and spoon on the right,
on the left place the fork.
Help set the table tonight!

(Oh bother, forgot the cup . . .
above the knife is where it goes.
A cup is useful for drinking,
but that part everyone knows.)

At the Table

"Happy birthday, Roo!" cheered Pooh.

All the Hundred-Acre friends gathered around the picnic table. It was time for Roo to blow out the candles on his cake.

"Can I help ya, Roo Boy?" asked Tigger excitedly.

"Of course, Tigger," said Roo.

WHOOSH! All the little flames were gone—and so was Roo's new party hat.

While Kanga cut the cake, Roo passed to Pooh a plate piled high with cookies.

"Mmm, honey cookies are my favorite," said Pooh. "Thank you." He put his napkin on his lap and waited for everyone to be seated and served. Then he began to eat the cookies.

Eeyore watched Pooh munching the cookies. "Don't worry about me," he rumbled. "No one ever does."

"Excuse me, Pooh," said Piglet quietly. "I think you are supposed to pass that plate of cookies."

"Oh, yes," said Pooh quickly. "It's just that the plate was
a little . . . heavy for passing. It's much lighter now." He
passed the plate to Eeyore.

"Very thoughtful, Pooh Bear," said Eeyore. "Not like some."

Eeyore ate a tasty cookie and passed the plate along. Then Kanga brought out a plate of crunchy thistles, just for him.

"Have you ever tried them with a little salt?" suggested Kanga. Christopher Robin passed the salt and pepper shakers.

"Is he putting the pepper on, too?" asked Piglet. Pepper sometimes tickled Piglet's nose in an "achoo-achoo" sort of way.

"No, but the salt always prefers to travel with someone," said Christopher Robin.

"Just like me," said Piglet.

By now Pooh had spied a jar of tasty honey. The jar was right in the middle in the table, and soon that's where Pooh was, too.

"Would you like me to pass the honey?" asked Christopher Robin.

"Oh no," said Pooh. "I can reach it nicely right here."

"But no one else can reach their food," pointed out
Christopher Robin.

Pooh clambered back into his seat. After a moment, he
said, "Christopher Robin, I've had a thought. It's probably

not a very good one. But I was thinking that you
could pass me the honey."

"That's a very good thought, Pooh Bear. A very-
good-manners kind of thought. Here you go," said
Christopher Robin, passing the jar.

Now, when the other friends heard Pooh Bear getting
a compliment on his good manners, they all wanted a
compliment, too.

"I-I used my napkin to clean my mouth," blurted Piglet.
"I didn't use my shirt. Or anyone else's."

"I've been savin' up all my extry-bounciness for after eatin'," added Tigger.

"I covered my mouth when I coughed," said Eeyore,
"if that's good enough for good manners—which I doubt."

"I took just the amount of food I knew I could eat," said Rabbit. "I would have mentioned it earlier, but I never talk with my mouth full."

"Say, that's double manners, Long-Ears," said Tigger.

"Well, if you say so, Tigger," said Rabbit, looking quite pleased.

"And I ate some of Rabbit's salad, even though I don't like salad," piped up Roo.

"Roo, dear!" said Mrs. Kanga.

"Well, I don't *usually* like it," replied Roo, more quietly.

"Following my Uncle Clarence's advice, my posture has remained perfectly perpendicular," said Owl.

"What's that you say, Beak Lips?" asked Tigger.

"I've been sitting up straight," said Owl.

"You all have shown wonderful manners," said Christopher Robin. "Parties are friendlier with manners, don't you think?" Everyone agreed.

Next, Kanga carried out a tray of small bowls. "I hope you all like my special ice cream soup," she said. "It's Roo's favorite."

"I'd better stir it to cool it down," said Eeyore, turning his spoon through his bowl. He was pleased to know that it's

not good manners to blow on hot soup to cool it.

"But ice cream soup is quite cool," said Kanga.

"Just goes to show," said Eeyore gloomily, "no one keeps me informed."

"SLURP!" slurped Tigger. "This ice cream soup is terrifically terrific, Mrs. Kanga."

"Thank you, Tigger," said Kanga.

Tigger noticed that the loudest slurping was coming from him. Then he noticed that the only slurping was coming from him!

Tigger peeked at Christopher Robin eating his soup:

he tipped the spoon away from him and filled it by moving
it toward the outside of the soup bowl.

He used the side of his spoon to cut the larger ice cream bits. Tigger copied him.

So that's how to eat extry quiet-like, discovered Tigger.

Next to Tigger, Kanga was telling Roo, "Don't play with your food, dear."

"But Mama, these licorices are playing with me," said Roo.

Kanga showed Roo how to roll long licorices onto his fork, a few strands at a time. "Just bite off the extra-long ends," she explained.

At last, most of Kanga's tasty treats had been eaten. "May I please be excused, Mama?" asked Roo.

"Have you all had enough?" Kanga asked her guests.

Without really meaning to, everyone peeked over at Pooh, who nodded and said, "Yes, I've had enough, thank you." Which the friends were happy to hear, because they were all ready to play.

Everyone helped Kanga clean up, and then there were games of tag and hide-and-seek. No one could find Pooh until his after-dinner-snoozing snores gave away his hiding spot.

When it was time to go, Pooh told Kanga and Roo, "Thank you for inviting me."

"We're so glad you could come, dear," said Kanga.

"We saved this extra pot of honey just for you, Pooh
Bear," said Roo, handing his friend a nearly full honeypot.
"Thank you very much!" said Pooh.

Pooh was surprised to get a gift when it wasn't even his birthday. But then, getting a gift made it feel like his birthday, which was such a happy feeling that Pooh began to hum as he walked home alongside Christopher Robin.

Yum-yum, when you're out eating with friends,
share the food and the drinks and the fun.
But keep noises and bumping and bouncing for later,
and it's nicer for everyone. Hum-de-dum!

Tramping through the golden Hundred-Acre Wood afternoon, Christopher Robin and Pooh soon found themselves back at Pooh's home.

Pooh sighed happily. "I think I used all my manners today," said Pooh. "My Visiting, Playing, Getting Ready, Setting the Table, and At the Table—Not On the Table—manners."

"Silly old bear," said Christopher Robin lovingly. "Manners come up everywhere and all the time."

"Ah," said Pooh wisely. "You never can tell with manners."

"First thing in the morning, I had to use my telephone manners," said Christopher Robin.

"I don't have a telephone," said Pooh sadly, "so I must not have any telephone manners."

"We can practice, Pooh," suggested Christopher Robin. "Even without a telephone." He picked up one of Pooh's cups. "Ring-ring!"

Pooh picked up a cup.

"When you pick up a ringing telephone, you say hello and your name," explained Christopher Robin.

"Hello and your name," repeated Pooh.

"I have a better idea," said Christopher Robin. "You can say, "Hello, it's Winnie the Pooh."

"That does make more sense," agreed Pooh. "Hello, it's Winnie the Pooh," he said into his cup.

"Now you say, 'May I ask who's calling?'" said Christopher Robin.

"May I ask who's calling?" said Pooh.

"Well done, Pooh. Now that we know who we are, we can talk. Or I might ask to speak to someone else."

"But there isn't anyone else here," said Pooh, confused.

"You don't need to let the caller know that no one else is here, but you can offer to take a message," said Christopher Robin. Christopher Robin took out a piece of paper. "You

write down the name of the caller, the time of the call, and the reason for calling."

Christopher Robin wrote out a note and read it to Pooh:

Christopher Robin
called for Piglet.
4:00 PM
Will be visiting
tomorrow.

"That's a useful sort of note," said Pooh.

"It's most useful once you give it to the person it's for," said Christopher Robin.

"I'll go give it right to Piglet," said Pooh eagerly.

"This is just a pretend note," reminded Christopher Robin. (The note looked quite real to Pooh, but he didn't want to say so.)

"So now do I know every manner?" asked Pooh.

"Different manners come up all the time," began Christopher Robin. "You should ask before you borrow something, and return it promptly. Cover your mouth if you're sneezing or yawning. Give your seat to someone who needs it. Say you're sorry if you break someone's toy, and offer to replace it . . ."

"Ask before you break something," repeated Pooh. "Give your sneeze to someone who needs it. Cover your seat before you're sorry . . . oh bother!" The rules seemed to be getting turned in and out, and a little backward, too.

"There's really only one rule about manners," said
Christopher Robin kindly. "And that's to treat others as
you like to be treated. That's not too hard to remember,
is it, Pooh Bear?"

"As you like to be treated is how you treat others," said Pooh. And even though it came out a little wobbly, it still sounded right. Then Pooh hummed a brand-new hum about manners, and that sounded right, too.

There are lots of words that make good manners,

like "Excuse me," "Well done," and

"Please pass the honey—er, bananas."

But if you forget the words—

spelling, size, or amount—

just remember:

It's the kindness that counts.

Evening was settling over Pooh's home in his cozy corner of the Wood. And there was something about that time of day that made Pooh think it was the perfect time for a little something.

Happily he reached into the honeypot that Kanga and Roo had given him. "Would you like some honey?" Pooh asked Christopher Robin.

"No, thank you," said Christopher Robin. After a moment, he added, "It was friendly of Kanga and Roo to give you a present."

"That's just what I thought, too," said Pooh in a rather

sticky voice. "I thanked them very much."

"After it's time for a little something, it might be time to write them a thank-you note," suggested Christopher Robin. "It's the thing to do when you get presents."

"What kinds of presents do I write notes for?" asked
Pooh.

"Every kind," said Christopher Robin.

"Even if the present isn't a honeypot?" asked Pooh.

"Or a smackerel of honey? Or any kind of honey at all?"

"Even then," said Christopher Robin. "When you write your note, you're not just thinking about your present—but also about the friend who gave it to you."

"But what if my writing is a little wobbly?" asked Pooh. Sometimes his letters did not come out in the right order or shape.

"If you tell me what you want to say, I can write it down," offered Christopher Robin. "Then you can decorate it yourself."

"Thank you," said Pooh.

"You're welcome," said Christopher Robin.

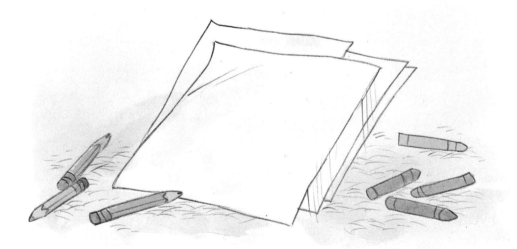

Pooh recited:

"Well done," said Christopher Robin.

Pooh decorated the note. And as he was walking to his mailbox, he began to hum.

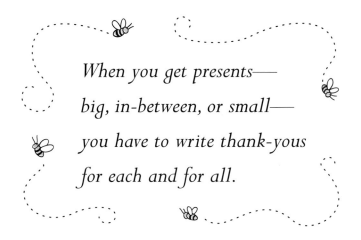

When you get presents—

big, in-between, or small—

you have to write thank-yous

for each and for all.